The Tiger Rising

The Tiger
Rising

Kate DiCamillo

CANDLEWICK PRESS
CAMBRIDGE, MASSACHUSETTS

Copyright © 2001 by Kate DiCamillo

First paperback edition 2002

The Library of Congress has cataloged the hardcover edition as follows:

DiCamillo, Kate.
The tiger rising/Kate DiCamillo. —1st ed.
p.   cm.
Summary: Rob, who passes the time in his rural
Florida community by wood carving, is drawn by his
spunky but angry friend Sistine into a plan to
free a caged tiger.
ISBN 0-7636-0911-0 (hardcover)
[1. Tigers—Fiction. 2. Animals—Treatment—Fiction.
3. Wood carving—Fiction. 4. Friendship—Fiction.
5. Florida—Fiction.] I. Title.
PZ7.D54156 Ti 2001   [Fic]—dc21   99-088635

ISBN 0-7636-1898-5 (paperback)

6 8 10 9 7

Printed in the United States of America

This book was typeset in Garamond.

Candlewick Press
2067 Massachusetts Avenue
Cambridge, Massachusetts 02140

visit us at www.candlewick.com

For my brother

I am grateful to Matt Pogatshnik

for giving me the music,

Bill Mockler for always reading,

the McKnight Foundation

for bestowing peace of mind,

Jane Resh Thomas for shining a

light on the path, Tracey Bailey

and Lisa Beck for being my

"death of the hired man" friends,

my mother for telling me not

to give up, and to Kara LaReau

for believing that I could . . .

and that I can. And that I will.

1

That morning, after he discovered the tiger, Rob went and stood under the Kentucky Star Motel sign and waited for the school bus just like it was any other day. The Kentucky Star sign was composed of a yellow neon star that rose and fell over a piece of blue neon in the shape of the state of Kentucky. Rob liked the sign; he harbored a dim but abiding notion that it would bring him good luck.

Finding the tiger had been luck, he knew that. He had been out in the woods behind the Kentucky Star Motel, way out in the woods, not really looking for anything, just wandering, hoping that maybe he would get lost or get eaten by a bear and not have to go to school ever again. That's when he saw the old Beauchamp gas station building, all boarded up and tumbling down; next to it, there was a cage, and inside the cage, unbelievably, there was a tiger—

a real-life, very large tiger pacing back and forth. He was orange and gold and so bright, it was like staring at the sun itself, angry and trapped in a cage.

It was early morning and it looked like it might rain; it had been raining every day for almost two weeks. The sky was gray and the air was thick and still. Fog was hugging the ground. To Rob, it seemed as if the tiger was some magic trick, rising out of the mist. He was so astounded at his discovery, so amazed, that he stood and stared. But only for a minute; he was afraid to look at the tiger for too long, afraid that the tiger would disappear. He stared, and then he turned and ran back into the woods, toward the Kentucky Star. And the whole way home, while his brain doubted what he had seen, his heart beat out the truth to him. *Ti-ger. Ti-ger. Ti-ger.*

That was what Rob thought about as he stood beneath the Kentucky Star sign and waited for the bus. The tiger. He did not think about the rash on his legs, the itchy red blisters that snaked their way into his shoes. His father said that it would be less likely to itch if he didn't think about it.

And he did not think about his mother. He hadn't thought about her since the morning of the funeral, the morning he couldn't stop crying the great heaving sobs that made his chest and stomach hurt. His father, watching him, standing beside him, had started to cry, too.

They were both dressed up in suits that day; his father's suit was too small. And when he slapped Rob to make him stop crying, he ripped a hole underneath the arm of his jacket.

"There ain't no point in crying," his father had said afterward. "Crying ain't going to bring her back."

It had been six months since that day, six months since he and his father had moved from Jacksonville to Lister, and Rob had not cried since, not once.

The final thing he did not think about that morning was getting onto the bus. He specifically did not think about Norton and Billy Threemonger waiting for him like chained and starved guard dogs, eager to attack.

Rob had a way of not-thinking about things. He imagined himself as a suitcase that was too full, like the one that he had packed when they left Jacksonville after the funeral. He made all his feelings go inside the suitcase; he stuffed them in tight and then sat on the suitcase and locked it shut. That was the way he not-thought about things. Sometimes it was hard to keep the suitcase shut. But now he had something to put on top of it. The tiger.

So as he waited for the bus under the Kentucky Star sign, and as the first drops of rain fell from the sullen sky, Rob imagined the tiger on top of his suitcase, blinking his golden eyes, sitting proud and strong, unaffected by all the not-thoughts inside straining to come out.

2

"Looky here," said Norton Threemonger as soon as Rob stepped onto the school bus. "It's the Kentucky Star. How's it feel to be a star?" Norton stood in the center of the aisle, blocking Rob's path.

Rob shrugged.

"Oh, he don't know." Norton called to his brother. "Hey, Billy, he don't know what it's like to be a star."

Rob slipped past Norton. He walked all the way to the back of the bus and sat down in the last seat.

"Hey," said Billy Threemonger, "you know what? This ain't Kentucky. This is Florida."

He followed Rob and sat down right next to him. He pushed his face so close that Rob could smell his breath. It was bad breath. It smelled metallic and rotten. "You ain't a Kentucky star," Billy said, his eyes glowing under the brim of his John Deere cap.

"And you sure ain't a star here in Florida. You ain't a star nowhere."

"Okay," said Rob.

Billy shoved him hard. And then Norton came swaggering back and leaned over Billy and grabbed hold of Rob's hair with one hand, and with the other hand, ground his knuckles into Rob's scalp.

Rob sat there and took it. If he fought back, it lasted longer. If he didn't fight back, sometimes they got bored and left him alone. They were the only three kids on the bus until it got into town, and Mr. Nelson, the driver, pretended like he didn't know what was going on. He drove staring straight ahead, whistling songs that didn't have any melody. Rob was on his own, and he knew it.

"He's got the creeping crud all over him," said Billy. He pointed at Rob's legs. "Look," he said to Norton. "Ain't it gross?"

"Uh-huh," said Norton. He was concentrating on grinding his knuckles into Rob's head. It hurt, but Rob didn't cry. He never cried. He was a pro at not-crying. He was the best not-crier in the world. It drove Norton and Billy Threemonger wild. And today, Rob had the extra power of the tiger. All he had to do was think about it, and he knew there was no way he would cry. Not ever.

They were still out in the country, only halfway into town, when the bus lurched to a stop. This was such a surprising development, to have the bus stop halfway through its route, that Norton stopped grinding his knuckles into Rob's scalp and Billy stopped punching Rob in the arm.

"Hey, Mr. Nelson," Norton shouted. "Whatcha doin'?"

"This ain't a stop, Mr. Nelson," Billy called out helpfully.

But Mr. Nelson ignored them. He kept whistling his non-song as he swung open the bus door. And while Norton and Billy and Rob watched, open-mouthed and silent, a girl with yellow hair and a pink lacy dress walked up the steps and onto the bus.

3

Nobody wore pink lacy dresses to school. Nobody. Even Rob knew that. He held his breath as he watched the girl walk down the aisle of the bus. Here was somebody even stranger than he was. He was sure.

"Hey," Norton called, "this is a school bus."

"I know it," the girl said. Her voice was gravelly and deep, and the words sounded clipped and strange, like she was stamping each one of them out with a cookie cutter.

"You're all dressed up to go to a party," Billy said. "This ain't the party bus." He elbowed Rob in the ribs.

"Haw." Norton laughed. He gave Rob a friendly thud on the head.

The girl stood in the center of the aisle, swaying with the movement of the bus. She stared at them.

"It's not my fault you don't have good clothes," she said finally. She sat down and put her back to them.

"Hey," said Norton. "We're sorry. We didn't mean nothing. Hey," he said again. "What's your name?"

The girl turned and looked at them. She had a sharp nose and a sharp chin and black, black eyes.

"Sistine," she said.

"Sistine," hooted Billy. "What kind of stupid name is that?"

"Like the chapel," she said slowly, making each word clear and strong.

Rob stared at her, amazed.

"What are you looking at?" she said to him.

Rob shook his head.

"Yeah," said Norton. He cuffed Rob on the ear. "What are you staring at, disease boy? Come on," he said to Billy.

And together, they swaggered up the aisle of the bus and sat in the seat behind the new girl.

They whispered things to her, but Rob couldn't hear what they were saying. He thought about the Sistine Chapel. He had seen a picture of it in the big art book that Mrs. Dupree kept on a small shelf behind her desk in the library. The pages of the book were slick and shiny. And each picture made Rob feel cool and sweet inside, like a drink of water on a hot day. Mrs. Dupree let Rob look at the book because he was quiet and good in the library. It was her reward to him.

In the book, the picture from the ceiling of the Sistine Chapel showed God reaching out and touching Adam. It was like they were playing a game of tag, like God was making Adam "it." It was a beautiful picture.

Rob looked out the window at the gray rain and the gray sky and the gray highway. He thought about the tiger. He thought about God and Adam. And he thought about Sistine. He did not think about the rash. He did not think about his mother. And he did not think about Norton and Billy Threemonger. He kept the suitcase closed.

4

Sistine was in Rob's sixth-grade homeroom class. Mrs. Soames made her stand up and introduce herself.

"My name," she said in her gravelly voice, "is Sistine Bailey." She stood at the front of the room, in her pink dress. And all the kids stared at her with open mouths as if she had just stepped off a spaceship from another planet. Rob looked down at his desk. He knew not to stare at her. He started working on a drawing of the tiger.

"What a lovely name," said Mrs. Soames.

"Thank you," said Sistine.

Patrice Wilkins, who sat in front of Rob, snorted and then giggled and then covered her mouth.

"I'm from Philadelphia, Pennsylvania," Sistine said, "home of the Liberty Bell, and I hate the South because the people in it are ignorant. And I'm not staying here in Lister. My father is coming to get me next week." She looked around the room defiantly.

"Well," said Mrs. Soames, "thank you very much for introducing yourself, Sistine Bailey. You may take your seat before you put your foot in your mouth any farther."

The whole class laughed at that. Rob looked up just as Sistine sat down. She glared at him. Then she stuck her tongue out at him. *Him!* He shook his head and went back to his drawing.

He sketched out the tiger, but what he wanted to do was whittle it in wood. His mother had shown him how to whittle, how to take a piece of wood and make it come alive. She taught him when she was sick. He sat on the edge of the bed and watched her tiny white hands closely.

"Don't jiggle that bed," his father said. "Your mama's in a lot of pain."

"He ain't hurting me, Robert," his mother said.

"Don't get all tired out with that wood," his father said.

"It's all right," his mother said. "I'm just teaching Rob some things I know."

But she said she didn't have to teach him much. His mother told him he already knew what to do. His hands knew; that's what she said.

"Rob," said the teacher, "I need you to go to the principal's office."

Rob didn't hear her. He was working on the tiger, trying to remember what his eyes looked like.

"Robert," Mrs. Soames said. "Robert Horton." Rob looked up. Robert was his father's name. Robert was what his mother had called his father. "Mr. Phelmer wants to see you in his office. Do you understand?"

"Yes, ma'am," said Rob.

He got up and took his picture of the tiger and folded it up and put it in the back pocket of his shorts. On his way out of the classroom, Jason Uttmeir tripped him and said, "See you later, retard," and Sistine looked up at him with her tiny black eyes. She shot him a look of pure hate.

5

The principal's office was small and dark and smelled like pipe tobacco. The secretary looked up at Rob when he walked in. "Go right on back," she said, nodding her big blond head of hair. "He's waiting for you."

"Rob," said Mr. Phelmer when Rob stepped into his office.

"Yes, sir," said Rob.

"Have a seat," Mr. Phelmer said, waving his hand at the orange plastic chair in front of his desk.

Rob sat down.

Mr. Phelmer cleared his throat. He patted the piece of hair that was combed over his bald head. He cleared his throat again. "Rob, we're a bit worried," he finally said.

Rob nodded. This was how Mr. Phelmer began all his talks with Rob. He was always worried: worried that Rob did not interact with the other students, worried that he did not communicate, worried that he wasn't doing well, in any way, at school.

"It's about your, uh, legs. Yes. Your legs. Have you been putting that medicine on them?"

"Yes, sir," said Rob. He didn't look at Mr. Phelmer. He stared instead at the paneled wall behind the principal's head. It was covered with an astonishing array of framed pieces of paper—certificates and diplomas and thank-you letters.

"May I, uh, look?" asked Mr. Phelmer. He got up from his chair and came halfway around his desk and stared at Rob's legs.

"Well, sir," he said after a minute. He went back behind his desk and sat down. He folded his hands together and cracked his knuckles. He cleared his throat.

"Here's the situation, Rob. Some of the parents—I won't mention any names—are worried that what you've got there might be contagious, *contagious* meaning something that the other students could possibly catch." Mr. Phelmer cleared his throat again. He stared at Rob.

"Tell me the truth, son," he said. "Have you been using that medicine you told me about? The stuff that doctor in Jacksonville gave you? Have you been putting that on?"

"Yes, sir," said Rob.

"Well," said Mr. Phelmer, "let me tell you what I think. Let me be up-front and honest with you. I think it might be a good idea if we had you stay home for a few days. What we'll do is just give that old medicine more of a chance to kick in, let it start working its magic on you, and then we'll have you come back to school when your legs have cleared up. What do you think about that plan?"

Rob stared down at his legs. He felt the picture of the tiger burning in his pocket. He concentrated on keeping his heart from singing out loud with joy.

"Yes, sir," he said slowly, "that would be all right."

"That's right," said Mr. Phelmer. "I thought you would think it's a good plan. I'll tell you what I'll do. I'll just write your parents—I mean your father— a note, and tell him what's what; he can give me a call if he wants. We can talk about it."

"Yes, sir," said Rob again. He kept his head down. He was afraid to look up.

Mr. Phelmer cleared his throat and scratched his head and adjusted his piece of hair, and then he started to write.

When he was done, he handed the note to Rob; Rob took it, and when he was outside the principal's office, he folded the piece of paper up carefully and put it in his back pocket with the drawing of the tiger.

And then, finally, he smiled. He smiled because he knew something Mr. Phelmer did not know. He knew that his legs would never clear up.

He was free.

chapter

Rob floated through the rest of the morning. He went to math class and civics and science, his heart light, buoyed by the knowledge that he would never have to come back.

At lunch, he sat out on the benches in the breeze-way. He did not go into the lunchroom; Norton and Billy Threemonger were there. And nothing had tasted good to him since his mother died, especially not the food at the school. It was worse than the food his father tried to cook.

He sat on the bench and unfolded his drawing of the tiger, and his fingers itched to start making it in wood. He was sitting like that, swinging his legs, studying the drawing, when he heard shouting and the high-pitched buzz of excitement, like crickets, that the kids made when something was happening.

He stayed where he was. In a minute, the faded

red double doors of the lunchroom swung open and Sistine Bailey came marching through them, her head held high. Behind her was a whole group of kids, and just when Sistine noticed Rob sitting there on the bench, one of the kids threw something at her; Rob couldn't tell what. But it hit her, whatever it was.

"Run!" he wanted to yell at her. "Hurry up and run!"

But he didn't say anything. He knew better than to say anything. He just sat and stared at Sistine with his mouth open, and she stared back at him. Then she turned and walked back into the group of kids, like somebody walking into deep water.

And suddenly, she began swinging with her fists. She was kicking. She was twirling. Then the group of kids closed in around her and she seemed to disappear. Rob stood up so that he could see her better. He caught sight of her pink dress; it looked all crumpled, like a wadded-up tissue. He saw her arms still going like mad.

"Hey!" he shouted, not meaning to.

"Hey!" he shouted again louder. He moved closer, the drawing of the tiger still in his hand.

"Leave her alone!" he shouted, not believing that the words were coming from him.

They heard him then and turned to him. It was quiet for a minute.

"Who you talking to?" a big girl with black hair asked.

"Yeah," another girl said. "Who do you think you're talking to?"

"Go away," Sistine muttered in her gravelly voice. But she didn't look at him. Her yellow hair was stuck to her forehead with sweat.

The girl with the black hair pushed up close to him. She shoved him.

"Leave her alone," Rob said again.

"You going to make me?" the black-haired girl said.

They were all looking at him. Waiting. Sistine was waiting, too; waiting for him to do something. He looked down at the ground and saw what they had thrown at her. It was an apple. He stared at it for what seemed like a long time, and when he looked back up, they were all still waiting to see what he would do.

And so he ran. And after a minute, he could tell that they were running after him; he didn't need to look back to see if they were there. He knew it. He knew the feeling of being chased. He dropped the picture of the tiger and ran full out, pumping his legs and arms hard. They were still behind him. A sudden thrill went through him when he realized that what he was doing was saving Sistine Bailey.

Why he would try to save Sistine Bailey, why he would want to save somebody who hated him, he couldn't say. He just ran, and the bell rang before they caught him. He was late for his English class because he had to walk from the gym all the way to the front of the school. And he did not know where his drawing of the tiger was, but he still had Mr. Phelmer's note in his back pocket and that was all that truly mattered to him, the note that proved that he would never have to come back.

7

It turned out to be an extraordinary day in almost every possible way. It started with finding the tiger, and it ended with Sistine Bailey sitting down next to him on the bus on the way home from school. Her dress was torn and muddied. There was a scrape down her right arm, and her hair stuck out in a hundred different directions. She sat down in the empty seat beside him and stared at him with her black eyes.

"There isn't anyplace else to sit," she said to him. "This is the last empty seat."

Rob shrugged.

"It's not like I want to sit here," she said.

"Okay," said Rob. He shrugged his shoulders again. He hoped that she wasn't going to thank him for saving her.

"What's your name?" she demanded.

"Rob Horton," he told her.

"Well, let me tell you something, Rob Horton. You shouldn't run. That's what they want you to do. Run."

Rob stared at her with his mouth open. She stared back.

"I hate it here," she said, looking away from him, her voice even deeper than before. "This is a stupid hick town with stupid hick teachers. Nobody in the whole school even knows what the Sistine Chapel is."

"I know," said Rob. "I know what the Sistine Chapel is." Immediately, he regretted saying it. It was his policy not to say things, but it was a policy he was having a hard time maintaining around Sistine.

"I bet," Sistine sneered at him. "I bet you know."

"It's a picture of God making the world," he said.

Sistine stared at him hard. She narrowed her small eyes until they almost disappeared.

"It's in Italy," said Rob. "The pictures are painted on the ceiling. They're frescoes." It was as if a magician had cast a spell over him. He opened his mouth and the words fell out, one on top of the other, like gold coins. He couldn't stop talking. "I don't got to go to school on account of my legs. I got a note that says so. Mr. Phelmer—he's the principal—he says the parents are worried that what I got is contagious. That means that the other kids could catch it."

"I know what *contagious* means," Sistine said. She looked at his legs. And then she did something truly astounding: she closed her eyes and reached out her left hand and placed it on top of Rob's right leg.

"Please let me catch it," she whispered.

"You won't," said Rob, surprised at her hand, how small it was and how warm. It made him think, for a minute, of his mother's hand, tiny and soft. He stopped that thought. "It ain't contagious," he told her.

"Please let me catch it," Sistine whispered again, ignoring him, keeping her hand on his leg. "Please let me catch it so I won't have to go to school."

"It ain't a disease," said Rob. "It's just me."

"Shut up," Sistine said. She sat up very straight. Her lips moved. The other kids shouted and screamed and laughed and called to each other, but the two of them sat apart from it all, as if their seat was an island in the sea of sweat and exhaust.

Sistine opened her eyes. She took her hand away and rubbed it up and down both of her own legs.

"You're crazy," Rob told her.

"Where do you live?" Sistine asked, still rubbing her hand over her legs.

"In the motel. In the Kentucky Star."

"You live in a motel?" she said, looking up at him.

"It ain't permanent," he told her. "It's just until we get back on our feet."

Sistine stared at him. "I'll bring you your homework," she said. "I'll bring it to you at the motel."

"I don't want my homework," he told her.

"So?" said Sistine.

By then, Norton and Billy Threemonger had spotted them sitting together and they were moving in. Rob was relieved when the first thump came to the back of his head, because it meant that he wouldn't have to talk to Sistine anymore. It meant that he wouldn't end up saying too much, telling her about important things, like his mother or the tiger. He was glad, almost, that Norton and Billy were there to beat him into silence.

His father read the note from the principal slowly, putting his big finger under the words as if they were bugs he was trying to keep still. When he was finally done, he laid the letter on the table and rubbed his eyes with his fingers and sighed. The rain beat a sad rhythm on the roof of the motel.

"That stuff ain't nothing anybody else can catch," his father said.

"I know it," Rob told him.

"I already told that to that principal once before. I called up there and told him that."

"Yes, sir," said Rob.

His father sighed. He stopped rubbing his eyes and looked up at Rob. "You want to stay home?" he asked.

Rob nodded.

His father sighed again. "Maybe I'll make an

appointment, get one of them doctors to write down that what you got ain't catching. All right?"

"Yes, sir," said Rob.

"But I won't do it for a few days. I'll give you some time off."

"That would be all right," said Rob.

"You got to fight them, you know. Them boys. I know you don't want to. But you got to fight them, else they won't ever leave you alone."

Rob nodded. He saw Sistine twirling and punching and kicking, and the vision made him smile.

"In the meantime, you can help me out around here," his father said. "Do some of the maintenance-man work at the motel, do some sweeping and cleaning for me. Beauchamp's running me ragged. There ain't enough hours in the day to do everything that man wants done. Now go on and hand me that medicine."

His father slathered and slapped the fishy-smelling ointment on Rob's legs, and Rob concentrated on holding still.

"Do you think Beauchamp is the richest man in the world?" he asked his father.

"Naw," his father said. "He don't own but this one itty-bitty motel now. And the woods. He just likes to pretend he's rich is all. Why?"

"I was just wondering," said Rob. He was thinking

about the tiger pacing back and forth in the cage. He was certain that the tiger belonged to Beauchamp, and wouldn't you have to be the richest man in the world to own a tiger? Rob wanted, desperately, to go see the tiger again. But he was afraid that he had imagined the whole thing; he was afraid that the tiger might have disappeared with the morning mist.

"Can I go outside?" Rob asked when his father was done.

"Naw," his father said. "I don't want that medicine rained off you. It cost too much."

Rob was relieved, almost, that he had to stay inside. What if he went looking for the tiger and he was not there?

Rob's father cooked them macaroni and cheese for supper on the two-burner hot plate they kept on the table next to the TV. He boiled the macaroni too long and a lot of it stuck to the pan, so there weren't many noodles to go with the powdery cheese.

"Someday," he told Rob, "you and me will have a house with a real stove, and I'll do some good cooking then."

"This is good," Rob lied.

"You eat all you want. I ain't that hungry," his father told him.

After supper, his father fell asleep in the recliner, with his head thrown back and his mouth open. He snored, and his feet—big, with crooked toes—jerked and trembled. In between the snores, his stomach growled long and loud, as if he was the hungriest man in the world.

Rob sat on his bed and started to work on carving the tiger. He had a good piece of maple, and his knife was sharp, and in his mind he could see the tiger clearly. But something different came out of the wood. It wasn't a tiger at all. It was a person, with a sharp nose and small eyes and skinny legs. It wasn't until he started working on the dress that Rob realized he was carving Sistine.

He stopped for a minute and held the wood out in front of him and shook his head in wonder. It was just like his mother had always said: You could never tell what would come out of the wood. It did what it wanted and you just followed.

He stayed up late working on the carving, and when he finally fell asleep, he dreamed about the tiger, only it wasn't in a cage. It was free and running through the woods, and there was something on its back, but Rob couldn't tell what it was. As the tiger got closer and closer, Rob saw that the thing was

Sistine in her pink party dress. She was riding the tiger. In his dream, Rob waved to her and she waved back at him. But she didn't stop. She and the tiger kept going, past Rob, deeper and deeper into the woods.

9

His father woke him up at five-thirty the next morning.

"Come on, son," he said, shaking Rob's shoulder. "Come on; you're a working man now. You got to get up." He took his hand away and stood over Rob for a minute more, and then he left.

Rob heard the door to the motel room squeak open. He opened his eyes. The world was dark. The only light came from the falling Kentucky Star. Rob turned over in bed and pulled back the curtain and looked out the window at the sign. It was like having his own personal shooting star, but he didn't ever make a wish on it. He was afraid that if he started wishing, he might not be able to stop. In his suitcase of not-thoughts, there were also not-wishes. He kept the lid closed on them, too.

Rob leaned on his elbow and stared at the star

and listened to the rain gently drumming its fingers on the roof. There was a warm glowing kind of feeling in his stomach, a feeling that he wasn't used to. It took him a minute to name it. The tiger. The tiger was out there. He got out of bed and put on shorts and a T-shirt.

"Still hot," his father said, when Rob stepped out the door. "And still raining."

"Uh-huh," said Rob, rubbing his eyes, "yes, sir."

"If it don't stop soon, the whole state ain't going to be nothing but one big swamp."

"The rain don't bother me," Rob muttered.

On the day of his mother's funeral, it had been so sunshiny that it hurt his eyes. And after the funeral, he and his father had to stand outside in the hot, bright light and shake everybody's hand. Some of the ladies hugged Rob, pulling him to them in jerky, desperate movements, smashing his head into their pillowy chests.

"If you don't look just like her," they told him, rocking him back and forth and holding on to him tight.

Or they said, "You got your mama's hair—that cobwebby blond," and they ran their fingers through his hair and patted his head like he was a dog.

And every time Rob's father extended his hand

to somebody else, Rob saw the ripped place in his suit, where it had split open when he slapped Rob to make him stop crying. And it reminded Rob again: *Do not cry. Do not cry.*

That was what the sun made him think of. The funeral. And so he didn't care if he ever saw the sun again. He didn't care if the whole state *did* turn into a swamp.

His father stood up and went back into the motel room and got himself a cup of coffee and brought it back outside. The steam rose off of it and curled into the air.

"Now that I'm a working man," Rob said shyly, "could I drink some coffee?"

His father smiled at him. "Well," he said, "I guess that'd be all right."

Rob went inside and poured himself a mug of coffee and brought it back outside and sat down next to his father and sipped it slowly. It tasted hot and dark and bitter. He liked it.

"All right," his father said after about ten minutes, "it's time to get to work." He stood up. It wasn't even six o'clock.

As they walked together alongside the back of the motel to the maintenance shed, his father started to whistle "Mining for Gold." It was a sad song he used to sing with Rob's mother. Her high sweet voice had gone swooping over his father's deep one, like a small bird flying over the solid world.

His father must have remembered, too, because he stopped halfway through the song and shook his head and cursed softly under his breath.

Rob let his father walk ahead of him. He slowed down and stared into the woods, wanting to see some small part of the tiger, a flick of his tail or the glow from his eyes. But there was nothing to see except for rain and darkness.

"Come on, son," his father said, his voice hard. And Rob hurried to catch up.

10

Rob was sweeping the laundry room when Willie May, the Kentucky Star's housekeeper, came in and threw herself down in one of the metal chairs that were lined up against the cement-block wall.

"You know what?" she said to Rob.

"No, ma'am," said Rob.

"I tell you what," said Willie May. She reached up and adjusted the butterfly clip in her thick black hair. "I'd rather be sweeping up after some pigs in a barn than cleaning up after the people in this place. Pigs at least give you some respect."

Rob leaned on his broom and stared at Willie May. He liked looking at her. Her face was smooth and dark, like a beautiful piece of wood. And Rob liked to think that if he had been the one who carved Willie May, he would have made her just the way she was, with her long nose and high cheekbones and slanted eyes.

"What you staring at?" Willie May asked. Her eyes narrowed. "What you doing out of school?"

Rob shrugged. "I don't know," he said.

"What you mean, you don't know?"

Rob shrugged again.

"Don't be moving your shoulders up and down in front of me, acting like some skinny old bird trying to fly away. You want to end up cleaning motel rooms for a living?"

Rob shook his head.

"That's right. Ain't nobody wants this job. I'm the only fool Beauchamp can pay to do it. You got to stay in school," she said, "else you'll end up like me." She shook her head and reached into the pocket of her dress and pulled out a single cigarette and two sticks of Eight Ball licorice gum. She put one piece of gum in her mouth, handed the other one to Rob, lit her cigarette, leaned back in the chair and closed her eyes. "Now," she said. The scent of smoke and licorice slowly filled the laundry room. "Go on and tell me why you ain't in school."

"On account of my legs being all broke out," said Rob.

Willie May opened her eyes and looked over the top of her glasses at Rob's legs.

"Mmmm," she said after a minute. "How long you had that?"

"About six months," said Rob.

"I can tell you how to cure that," said Willie May, pointing with her cigarette at his legs. "I can tell you right now. Don't need to go to no doctor."

"Huh?" said Rob. He stopped chewing his gum and held his breath. What if Willie May healed him and then he had to go back to school?

"Sadness," said Willie May, closing her eyes and nodding her head. "You keeping all that sadness down low, in your legs. You not letting it get up to your heart, where it belongs. You got to let that sadness rise on up."

"Oh," said Rob. He let his breath out. He was relieved. Willie May was wrong. She couldn't cure him.

"The principal thinks it's contagious," he said.

"Man ain't got no sense," Willie May said.

"He's got lots of certificates," Rob offered. "They're all framed and hung up on his wall."

"I bet he ain't got no certificate for sense though," said Willie May darkly. She rose up out of her chair and stretched. "I got to clean some rooms," she said. "You ain't going to forget what I told you 'bout them legs, are you?"

"No, ma'am," said Rob.

"What'd I tell you then?" she said, towering over him. Willie May was tall, the tallest person Rob had ever seen.

"To let the sadness rise," Rob said. He repeated the words as if they were part of a poem. He gave them a certain rhythm, the same way Willie May had when she said them.

"That's right," said Willie May. "You got to let the sadness rise on up."

She left the room in a swirl of licorice and smoke; after she was gone, Rob wished that he had told her about the tiger. He felt a sudden desperate need to tell somebody—somebody who wouldn't doubt him. Somebody who was capable of believing in tigers.

11

That afternoon, Rob was out in front of the Kentucky Star, weeding between the cracks in the sidewalk, when the school bus rumbled up.

"Hey!" he heard Norton Threemonger yell.

Rob didn't look up. He concentrated on the weeds.

"Hey, disease boy!" Norton shouted. "We know what you got. It's called leprosy."

"Yeah!" Billy shouted. "Leprosy. All of your body parts are going to fall off."

"They're going to *rot* off!" Norton yelled.

"Yeah!" Billy screamed. "That's what I meant. *Rot*. They're going to rot off."

Rob stared at the sidewalk and imagined the tiger eating Norton and Billy Threemonger and then spitting out their bones.

"Hey!" Norton shouted. "Here comes your girlfriend, disease boy."

The bus coughed and sputtered and finally roared away. Rob looked up. Sistine was walking toward him. She was wearing a lime green dress. As she got closer, he could see that it was torn and dirty.

"I brought your homework," she said. She held out a red notebook stuffed full of papers. The knuckles on her hand were bleeding.

"Thank you," said Rob. He took the notebook. He was determined to say nothing else to her. He was determined to keep his words inside himself, where they belonged.

Sistine stared past him at the motel. It was an ugly two-story building, squat and small, composed entirely of cement block. The doors of each room were painted a different color, pink or blue or green, and there was a chair, painted in a matching color, sitting in front of each door.

"Why is this place called the Kentucky Star?" Sistine asked.

"Because," said Rob. It was the shortest answer he could think of.

"Because why?" she asked.

Rob sighed. "Because Beauchamp, the man who owns it, he had a horse once, called Kentucky Star."

"Well," said Sistine, "it's a stupid name for a hotel in Florida."

Rob shrugged.

It started to rain; Sistine stood in front of him and continued to stare. She looked at the motel and then over at the blinking Kentucky Star sign, and then she looked back at him, as if it was all a math equation she was trying to make come out right in her head.

The rain made her hair stick to her scalp. It made her dress droopy. Rob looked at her small pinched face and her bleeding knuckles and dark eyes, and he felt something inside of him open up. It was the same way he felt when he picked up a piece of wood and started working on it, not knowing what it would be and then watching it turn into something he recognized.

He took a breath. He opened his mouth and let the words fall out. "I know where there's a tiger."

Sistine stood in the drizzly rain and stared at him, her eyes black and fierce.

She didn't say "A real one?"

She didn't say "Are you crazy?"

She didn't say "You're a big old liar."

She said one word: *"Where?"*

And Rob knew then that he had picked the right person to tell.

12

"We got to walk through the woods," Rob said. He looked doubtfully at Sistine's bright dress and shiny black shoes.

"You can give me some of your clothes to wear," she told him. "I hate this dress, anyway."

And so he took her to the motel room, and there, Sistine stood and stared at the unmade beds and the tattered recliner. Her eyes moved over his father's gun case and then went to the macaroni pan from the night before, still sitting on the hot plate. She looked at it all the same way she had looked at the Kentucky Star sign and the motel and him, like she was trying to add it up in her head.

Then she saw his carvings, the little wooden village of odd things that he had made. He had them all on a TV dinner tray beside his bed.

"Oh," she said—her voice sounded different, lighter—"where did you get those?"

She went and bent over the tray and studied the carvings, the blue jay and the pine tree and the Kentucky Star sign and the one that he was particularly proud of, his father's right foot, life-size and accurate right down to the little toe. She picked them up one by one and then placed them back down carefully.

"Where did you get them?" she asked again.

"I made 'em," said Rob.

She did not doubt him, as some people would. Instead, she said, "Michelangelo—the man who painted the Sistine ceiling—he sculpted, too. You're a sculptor," she said. "You're an artist."

"Naw," said Rob. He shook his head. He felt a hot wave of embarrassment and joy roll over him. It lit his rash on fire. He bent and rubbed his hands down his legs, trying to calm them. When he straightened back up, he saw that Sistine had picked up the carving of her. He had left it lying on his bed, intending to work on it again in the evening.

He held his breath as she stared at the piece of wood. It looked so much like her, with her skinny legs and small eyes and defiant stance, that he was

certain she would be angry. But once again she surprised him.

"Oh," she said, her voice full of wonder, "it's
perfect. It's like looking in a little wooden mirror."
She stared at it a minute more and then carefully laid
it back on his bed.

"Give me some clothes," she said, "and we'll go
see the tiger."

He gave her a pair of pants and a T-shirt, and left
the room and went outside to wait for her.

It was still raining, but not hard. He looked at
the falling Kentucky Star. He thought for a minute
about one of the not-wishes he had buried deepest:
a friend. He stared at the star and felt the hope and
need and fear course through him in a hot neon arc.
He shook his head.

"Naw," he said to the Kentucky Star. "Naw."

And then he sighed and stuck his legs out into
the rain, hoping to cool them off, hoping to get some
small amount of relief.

13

They walked together through the scrub. The rain had stopped, but the whole world was wet. The pines and the palmettos and the sad clusters of dead orange trees all dripped water.

"This is where my mother grew up," Sistine said, swinging her arms wide as she walked. "Right here in Lister. And she said that she always told herself that if she ever made it out of here, she wasn't going to come back. But now she's back because my father had an affair with his secretary, whose name is Bridgette and who can't type, which is a really bad thing for a secretary not to be able to do. And my mother left him when she found out. He's coming down here to get me. Soon. Next week, probably. I'm going to live with him. I'm not staying here, that's for sure."

Rob felt a familiar loneliness rise up and drape

its arm over his shoulder. She wasn't staying. There was no point in wishing; the suitcase needed to stay closed. He stared at Sistine's shiny shoes and willed his sadness to go away.

"Ain't you worried about messing up your shoes?" he asked her.

"No," she said, "I hate these shoes. I hate every piece of clothing that my mother makes me wear. Does your mother live with you?"

Rob shook his head. "Naw," he said.

"Where is she?"

Rob shrugged his shoulders.

"My mother's going to open up a store downtown. It's going to be an art store. She's going to bring some culture to the area. She could sell some of your wood sculptures."

"They ain't sculptures," Rob protested. "They're just whittling. That's all. And we got to be quiet because Beauchamp don't want people walking around on his land."

"Is this his land?" Sistine asked.

"Everything's his," said Rob. "The motel and these woods."

"He can't own everything," Sistine argued. "Besides," she said, "I don't care. He can catch us. He can put us in jail for trespassing. I don't care."

"If we're in jail, we won't get to see the tiger," said Rob.

"Where's your mother?" Sistine demanded suddenly. She stopped walking and stared at him.

"Shhh," said Rob. "You got to be quiet." He kept walking.

"I do not have to be quiet," Sistine called after him. "I want to know where your mother is."

He turned around and looked at her. Her hands were on her hips. Her black eyes were narrowed.

"I don't want to see your stupid tiger!" she shouted. "I don't care about it. You don't know how to talk to people. I told you about my father and my mother and Bridgette, and you didn't say anything. You won't even tell me about your mother." Keeping her hands on her hips, she turned around and started marching back in the direction of the Kentucky Star. "Keep your stupid secrets!" she shouted. "Keep your stupid tiger, too. I don't care."

Rob watched her. Because she was wearing his jeans and his shirt, it was like looking into a funhouse mirror. It was like watching himself walk away. He shrugged and bent to scratch his legs. He told himself that he didn't care. He told himself that she was leaving soon, anyway.

But when he looked up and saw her getting

smaller and smaller, it reminded him of his dream. He remembered Sistine riding into the woods on the back of the tiger. And suddenly, he couldn't bear the thought of watching her disappear again.

"Wait up!" he shouted. "Wait up!" And he started to run toward her.

Sistine turned and stopped. She waited for him with her hands on her hips.

"Well?" she said when he got close to her.

"She's dead," he told her. The words came out in short, ragged gasps. "My mama's dead."

"Okay," said Sistine. She gave a quick, professional nod of her head. She stepped toward him. And Rob turned. And together they walked back in the other direction, toward the tiger.

14

The cage was made out of rusted chainlink fence; there was a wood board that served as a roof, and there was a chainlink door that was locked tight with three padlocks. Inside the cage, the tiger was still pacing back and forth, just as he had been the last time Rob saw him, as if he had never stopped pacing, or as if Rob had never gone away.

"Oh," said Sistine in the same voice that she had used when she saw Rob's carvings. "He's beautiful."

"Don't get too close," Rob ordered. "He might not like it if you stand too close."

But the tiger ignored them. He concentrated on pacing. He was so enormous and bright that it was hard to look directly at him.

"It's just like the poem says," Sistine breathed.

"What?" said Rob.

"That poem. The one that goes, 'Tiger, tiger,

burning bright, in the forests of the night.' That poem. It's just like that. He burns bright."

"Oh," said Rob. He nodded. He liked the fierce and beautiful way the words sounded. Just as he was getting ready to ask Sistine to say them again, she whirled around and faced him.

"What's he doing way out here?" she demanded.

Rob shrugged. "I don't know," he said. "He's Beauchamp's, I guess."

"Beauchamp's what?" said Sistine. "His pet?"

"I don't know," said Rob. "I just like looking at him. Maybe Beauchamp does, too. Maybe he just likes to come out here and look at him."

"That's selfish," said Sistine.

Rob shrugged.

"This isn't right, for this tiger to be in a cage. It's not right."

"We can't do nothing about it," Rob said.

"We could let him go," said Sistine. "We could set him free." She put her hands on her hips. It was a gesture that Rob had already come to recognize and be wary of.

"We can't," he said. "There's all them locks."

"We can saw through them."

"Naw," said Rob. The mere thought of letting the tiger go made his legs itch like crazy.

"We have to set him free," Sistine said, her voice loud and certain.

"Nuh-uh," said Rob. "It ain't our tiger to let go."

"It's our tiger to save," Sistine said fiercely.

The tiger stopped pacing. He pricked his ears back and forth, looking somewhere past Sistine and Rob.

"Shhh," said Rob.

The tiger cocked his head. All three of them listened.

"It's a car," said Rob. "A car's coming. It's Beauchamp. We got to go. Come on."

He grabbed her hand and pulled her into the woods. She ran with him. She let him hold on to her hand. It was an impossibly small and bony hand, as delicate as the skeleton of a baby bird.

They ran together, and Rob felt his heart move inside him—not from fear or exertion but from something else. It was as if his soul had grown and was pushing everything up higher in his body. It was an oddly familiar feeling, but he couldn't remember what it was called.

"Is he behind us?" Sistine asked breathlessly.

Rob shrugged; it was hard to move his shoulders up and down and keep hold of Sistine's hand at the same time.

Sistine said, "Stop shrugging your shoulders at me. I hate it. I hate the way you shrug all the time."

And that made Rob remember Willie May saying that when he shrugged he looked like a skinny bird trying to fly. It struck him as funny now. He laughed out loud at the thought of it. And without asking him what he was laughing about, without dropping his hand, without stopping, Sistine laughed, too.

Then Rob remembered the name of the feeling that was pushing up inside him, filling him full to overflowing. It was happiness. That was what it was called.

15

By the time they made it back to the motel parking lot, it was dark outside, and they were both laughing so hard that they could barely walk.

"Rob?" said his father. He was standing at the door to their room. The blue-gray light from inside seeped out around him.

"Yes, sir," said Rob. He dropped Sistine's hand. He stood up straight.

"Where you been?"

"Out in the woods."

"Did you finish up all them jobs I told you to do?"

"Yes, sir," said Rob.

"Who you got with you?" his father said, squinting into the darkness.

Sistine drew herself up tall.

"This is Sistine," said Rob.

"Uh-huh," said his father, still squinting. "You live around here?" he asked.

"For now," said Sistine.

"Your parents know you're out here?"

"I was going to call my mother," said Sistine.

"There's a pay phone down in the laundry room," said Rob's father.

"In the laundry room?" Sistine repeated, her voice full of disbelief. She put her hands on her hips.

"We don't got a phone in the room," Rob said to her softly.

"Good grief," said Sistine. "Well, can I have some change at least?"

Rob's father reached into his pants pocket and pulled out a handful of coins. He balanced the money in the palm of his hand, as if he was preparing to do a magic trick, and Rob stepped forward and took the coins from him and handed them to Sistine.

"You want me to go with you?" he asked her.

"No," she said. "I'll find it. Thank you very much."

"Rob," his father said as Sistine marched away, swinging her arms, "what's that girl doing in your clothes?"

"She had on a dress," Rob said. "It was too pretty to wear out in the woods."

"Come on in here," his father commanded. "Let's get that medicine on your legs."

"Yes, sir," said Rob. He walked toward the room slowly. His happiness had evaporated. His legs itched. And the motel room, he knew, would be as dark as a cave, lit only by the gray light of the TV.

When his mother was alive, the world had seemed full of light. The Christmas before she died, she had strung the outside of their house, in Jacksonville, with hundreds of white lights. Every night, the house lit up like a constellation, and they were all inside it together, the three of them. And they were happy.

Rob remembered, and as he remembered, he stepped into the motel room. He shook his head and scolded himself for opening his suitcase. Just thinking about all the things that were gone now seemed to make the darkness darker.

Rob sat out on the curb in front of the motel room
and waited for Sistine to come back from using the
phone. He had her green dress wrapped up in a grocery bag. He had tried to fold the dress up neatly,
but folding a dress turned out to be an impossible
task and he finally gave up. Now he held the bag out
and away from him, so that the grease from the medicine on his legs would not stain it.

He was relieved when Sistine finally walked
toward him out of the darkness. "Hey," he said.

"Hi." She sat down on the steps next to him.
"How come you don't have a phone?"

Rob shrugged. "Ain't got nobody to call, I guess."

"My mother's coming to get me," Sistine said.

Rob nodded. "Here's your dress." He handed her
the bag.

Sistine took it and then tilted her head to look

up at the sky. Rob looked up, too. The clouds had shifted, and there were clear patches where the stars shone through.

"I can see the Big Dipper," Sistine said. "I like looking up at things. So do my mom and dad. That's how they met. They were both looking up at the ceiling in the Sistine Chapel and they weren't watching where they were going and they bumped into each other. That's why I'm named Sistine."

"I like your name," said Rob shyly.

"I've seen the Sistine ceiling, too," she said. "They took me last year. Before Bridgette. When they were still in love."

"Does it look like the pictures?" Rob asked.

"Better," said Sistine. "It's like—I don't know— it's like looking at fireworks, kind of."

"Oh," said Rob.

"Maybe we could go to Italy sometime. And I could show you."

"That would be all right," said Rob. He smiled into the darkness.

"That tiger can't look up at the stars," said Sistine, her voice getting hard. "He's got that piece of wood over his head. He can't look up at all. We've got to let him go."

Rob was silent. He was hoping that if he didn't

answer her, she might go back to talking about the Sistine ceiling.

"How did your mother die?" she asked suddenly.

Rob sighed. He knew there was no point in trying not to answer. "Cancer," he said.

"What was her name?"

"I ain't supposed to talk about her," said Rob, closing his eyes to the stars and concentrating instead on his suitcase, working to keep it closed.

"Why not?" asked Sistine.

"Because. My dad says it don't do no good to talk about it. He says she's gone and she ain't coming back. That's why we moved here from Jacksonville. Because everybody always wanted to talk about her. We moved down here to get on with things."

There was the crunch of gravel. Rob opened his eyes in time to see the headlights of a car sweep over them.

"That's my mother," said Sistine. She stood up. "Quick," she said. "Tell me your mother's name."

Rob shook his head.

"Say it," she demanded.

"Caroline," Rob said softly, cracking his suitcase open and letting the word slip out.

Sistine gave him another businesslike nod of her

head. "Okay," she said. "I'll come back tomorrow. And we'll make our plans for letting the tiger go."

"Sissy?" called a voice. "Baby, what in the world? What in the world are you doing out here?"

Sistine's mother got out of the car and came walking toward them. She had on high heels, and she wobbled as she walked in the gravel parking lot of the Kentucky Star. Her hair was a lighter shade of yellow than Sistine's and piled up high. When she turned her head, Rob recognized Sistine's profile, her sharp chin and pointed nose, but the mouth was different, tighter.

"Good lord," said Mrs. Bailey to Sistine. "What have you got on?"

"Clothes," said Sistine.

"Sissy, you look like a hobo. Get in the car." She tapped her high-heeled foot on the gravel.

Sistine didn't move. She stood beside Rob.

"Well," said her mother when Sistine didn't move, "you must be Rob. What's your last name, Rob?"

"Horton," said Rob.

"Horton," said Mrs. Bailey. "Horton. Are you related to Seldon Horton, the congressman?"

"No, ma'am," said Rob. "I don't think so."

Mrs. Bailey's eyes flicked away from him and back to Sistine. "Baby," said Mrs. Bailey, "please get in the car."

When Sistine still didn't move, Mrs. Bailey sighed and looked back at Rob again. "She won't listen to a word I say," Mrs. Bailey told him. "Her father is the only one she'll listen to." And then under her breath she muttered, "Her father, the liar."

Sistine growled somewhere deep in her throat and stalked to the car and got in and slammed the door. "You're the liar!" she shouted from the back seat of the car. "You're the one who lies!"

"Jesus," said Mrs. Bailey. She shook her head and turned and walked back to the car without saying anything else to Rob.

Rob watched them pull away. He could see Sistine sitting in the back seat. Her shoulders were slumped.

A motel room door slammed. Somebody laughed. A dog barked once, short and high, and then stopped. And then there was silence.

"Caroline," Rob whispered into the darkness. "Caroline. Caroline. Caroline." The word was as sweet as forbidden candy on his tongue.

17

The next morning, Rob was helping Willie May in the laundry room. They were folding sheets and chewing Eight Ball gum.

All night, he had tossed and turned, scratching his legs and thinking about the tiger and what Sistine said, that he had to be set free. He had finally decided to get Willie May's opinion.

"You ever been to a zoo?" Rob asked her.

"One time," said Willie May. She cracked her gum. "Went to that zoo over in Sorley. Place stunk."

"Do you think them animals minded it? Being locked up?"

"Wasn't nobody asking them did they mind." Willie May pulled another sheet out of the dryer and snapped it open.

Rob tried again. "Do you think it's bad to keep animals locked up?"

Willie May looked at him over the top of her glasses. She stared at him hard.

Rob looked down at his feet.

"When I wasn't but little," said Willie May, "my daddy brought me a bird in a cage. It was a green parakeet bird. That bird was so small, I could hold it right in the palm of my hand." She draped the sheet over one shoulder and held out a cupped hand to show Rob. It looked, to him, like a hand big enough to hold the entire world.

"Held him in my hand. Could feel his little heart beating. He would look at me, cock his head this way and that. Called him Cricket, on account of him all the time singing."

"What happened to him?" Rob asked.

Willie May bent and took a pillowcase out of the dryer.

"Let him go," she said.

"You let him go?" Rob repeated, his heart sinking inside him like a stone.

"Couldn't stand seeing him locked up, so I let him go." She folded the pillowcase carefully.

"And then what happened?"

"I got beat by my daddy. He said I didn't do that bird no favor. Said all I did was give some snake its supper."

"So you never saw him again?" Rob asked.

"Nuh-uh," said Willie May. "But sometimes, he comes flying through my dreams, flitting about and singing." She shook her head and reached for the sheet on her shoulder. "Here," she said. "Go on and grab ahold of the other end. Help me fold this up."

Rob took hold of the sheet, and as it billowed out between them, a memory rose up before him: his father standing out in the yard, holding his gun up to the sky, taking aim at a bird.

"You think I can hit it?" his father said. "You think I can hit that itty-bitty bird?"

"Robert," his mother said, "what do you want to shoot that bird for?"

"To prove I can," said his father.

There was a single crack and the bird was suspended in midair, pinned for a moment to the sky with his father's bullet. Then it fell.

"Oh, Robert," his mother said.

It hurt the back of Rob's throat to think about that now, to think about the gun and his mother and the small *thud* the bird made when it hit the ground.

"I know something that's in a cage," said Rob, pushing the words past the tightness in his throat.

Willie May nodded her head, but she wasn't listening. She was looking past Rob, past the white sheet, past the laundry room, past the Kentucky Star.

"Who don't?" she said finally. "Who don't know something in a cage?"

After that, they folded the sheets in silence. Rob thought about the bird and how when he had finally found its small still-warm body, he had started to cry.

His father told him not to.

"It ain't nothing to cry over," he'd said. "It's just a bird."

18

Rob was sweeping the cement walkway in front of the Kentucky Star rooms when Beauchamp pulled up in his red jeep and honked the horn.

"Hey there," he hollered. Beauchamp was a large man with orange hair and an orange beard and a permanent toothpick in the side of his mouth. The toothpick waggled as he talked, as if it was trying to make a point of its own. "We got you on the payroll now, too?" Beauchamp shouted.

"No, sir," said Rob.

"All right," hooted Beauchamp. He hopped out of the jeep. "Got you working for free. That's what I like to hear."

"Yes, sir," said Rob.

"Ain't you supposed to be in school? Or you done graduated already?" The gold chains buried deep in Beauchamp's orange chest-hair winked at Rob.

"I'm sick," said Rob.

"Sick and tired of school, right?" He slapped Rob on the back. "Don't got a mama putting down the rules for you, do you? Get to make your own rules. Not me," said Beauchamp. He jerked his head in the direction of the motel office, where his mother, Ida Belle, worked the front desk.

He winked at Rob and then looked to the left, then right. "Look here," he said in a quieter voice. "I've got me a number of deals going on right now, a few more than I can properly handle. I wonder if a smart boy like yourself wouldn't be looking for a way to pick up some extra spending money."

He didn't wait for Rob to answer.

"Let me tell you what I got cooking. You like animals?"

Rob nodded.

"Course you do," said Beauchamp, nodding with him. "What boy don't? You like wild animals?"

Rob's heart skipped. He suddenly knew where Beauchamp was headed.

"I got me a wild animal," said Beauchamp. "I got me a wild animal like you would not believe. Right here on my own property. And I got some plans for him. Big plans. But in the meantime, he needs some taking care of, some daily maintenance. You following me, son?"

"Yes, sir," said Rob.

"All right," said Beauchamp. He slapped Rob on the shoulder again. "Why don't you climb on into this jeep and let me take you for a ride, show you what I'm talking about."

"I'm supposed to be sweeping," said Rob. He held up the broom.

"Says who?" said Beauchamp, suddenly angry. "Your daddy? He ain't the boss. *I'm* the boss. And if I say 'Let's go,' you say 'All right.' "

"All right," said Rob. He looked over his shoulder, wishing fervently that Willie May or his father would appear to save him from Beauchamp, knowing at the same time that he could not be saved, that he was on his own.

"Good," said Beauchamp. "Climb on up."

Rob climbed into the passenger seat. There was a big brown grocery bag at his feet.

"Go on and put that in the back," said Beauchamp as he swung into the driver's seat.

The bag was heavy and it stunk. Rob carefully put it on the floor in the back and then noticed his hands. There was blood on his fingers.

"That's just from the meat," said Beauchamp. "It won't hurt you none." He cranked the engine. It roared to life, and they went tearing around behind the Kentucky Star and into the woods. Beauchamp drove like he was crazy. He gunned for trees and then swerved away from them at the last minute, whooping and hollering the whole time.

"You ain't going to believe what I got to show you," Beauchamp hollered at him.

"No, sir," said Rob weakly.

"What?" Beauchamp shouted.

"No, sir," Rob shouted back. "I ain't going to believe it."

But he did believe it. He believed it with all his heart.

19

Beauchamp hit the brakes.

"We're almost there," he said. "You got to close your eyes so it's a surprise."

Rob closed his eyes and the jeep went forward slowly. "Don't cheat now," Beauchamp said. "Keep them eyes closed."

"Yes, sir," Rob said.

"All right," Beauchamp said finally. "Go on and open them up."

He had pulled the jeep up as close to the tiger cage as possible without driving right into it. "Tell me what you see," he crowed. "Tell me what is before your very eyes."

"A tiger," said Rob. He let his mouth drop open. He tried to look excited and amazed.

"Damn straight," said Beauchamp. "King of the jungle. And he's all mine."

"Wow," said Rob. "You own him?"

"That's right," said Beauchamp. "Fellow I know owed me some money. Paid me with a tiger. That's the way real men do business. In tigers. He come complete with the cage." The toothpick in the side of his mouth danced up and down; Beauchamp put a finger up to steady it into silence.

"What are you going to do with him?" Rob asked.

"I'm studying my options. I figure I could set him up out front of the Kentucky Star, have him draw me some more business into the motel."

The tiger stood and stared at Beauchamp. Beauchamp looked away from him. He tapped his thick fingers on the steering wheel.

"I also might just kill him," Beauchamp said, "and skin him and make me a tiger coat. I ain't made up my mind. He's a lot of work, I'll tell you that. He needs meat twice a day. That's where you come in. I need you to come out here and feed him. Two bucks every time you do it. How's that sound?"

Rob swallowed hard. "How do I get the meat in the cage?" he asked.

Beauchamp dug in his pocket and pulled out a set of keys. "With these," he said. He shook the keys and they gave a sad jingle. "Don't pay no attention to the big keys. They're for the locks on the door. Open them up and that tiger will get out and eat you for sure. You understand? I ought not to give you this whole set, but I know you won't open up that door. Right? You ain't no fool, right?"

Rob, terrified that keys to the cage existed and that they were about to be handed to him, nodded.

"See this tiny key?" Beauchamp said.

Rob nodded again.

"That's for the food door, right there." Beauchamp pointed at a small door at the bottom of the cage. "You just open that up and toss the meat in a piece at a time. Like this."

Beauchamp swung himself out of the jeep with a grunt. He reached in the back seat for the grocery bag, took out a piece of meat, bent over and unlocked the tiny door, opened it, and threw the meat in. The tiger leaped forward, and Beauchamp took a quick step backward, stumbling.

"That's all there is to it," he said, straightening up. His forehead was shiny with sweat, and his hands were trembling.

"What's the tiger's name?" Rob asked.

"Name?" said Beauchamp. "He ain't got a name. You got to name something before you toss it a piece of meat?"

Rob shrugged and blushed. He bent over to scratch his legs so that he wouldn't have to look at Beauchamp's sweaty, angry face.

"You want to get introduced proper?" said Beauchamp in a mocking voice. "Well then, get on out of the jeep."

Rob climbed down.

Beauchamp grabbed hold of the fence and shook it. The tiger looked up from his meat. His muzzle was red with blood; he stared at Beauchamp with a fierce look in his eyes that was familiar to Rob.

"Hey!" Beauchamp shouted. "You see this boy here?" He pointed at Rob. "He's your meal ticket. Not me. It's this boy. He's got the keys now. Understand? I don't got them no more. This boy's got them. He's your boy."

The tiger stared at Beauchamp a minute more, and then he slowly lowered his head and started back to work on the meat.

"Now you two know each other," said Beauchamp. He pulled a tattered bandanna from his pocket and wiped the sweat off his forehead.

On the hair-raising ride back to the Kentucky Star, Rob realized who the tiger's stare reminded him of. It was Sistine. He knew that when he told her he had the keys to the cage, her eyes would glow with the same fierce light. He knew that she would insist that now they had to let the tiger go.

20

The last thing Beauchamp said to him was, "Don't forget, now, this is our business deal. It don't concern nobody else. You take that bag of meat and hide it somewhere, and I'll bring you more meat tomorrow. In the meantime, you keep your mouth shut."

At three o'clock, the school bus pulled up, belching and gasping and sighing. Norton and Billy Three-monger started pelting Rob with date palms before the bus even came to a complete stop. The bus door opened and Sistine came running toward him, dodging the dates, looking as serious as a soldier on a battlefield.

"Let's go see the tiger," she shouted to him.

Rob was dismayed to see that she was still wearing his shirt and jeans.

"Where's your dress?" he blurted.

"In here," she said. She held up the same grocery bag he had given her the night before. "I changed as soon as I got out of the house. My mother doesn't know. I found a book in the library today and read about big cats. Do you know that panthers live in the woods here? We could set the tiger free, and he could live with them. Come on," she said. She started to run.

Rob ran, too. But the keys to the cage felt heavy in his pocket, and they bumped up against his leg and slowed him down so that Sistine beat him there. When he arrived, she was standing pressed up against the fence, her fingers wrapped in the chainlink.

"Tigers are an endangered species, you know," she said. "It's up to us to save him."

"Watch out he don't attack you," Rob said.

"He won't. Tigers only attack people if they're desperately hungry."

"Well, this one ain't hungry."

"How do you know?" Sistine asked, turning around and looking at him.

"Well," said Rob, "he ain't skinny, is he? He don't look starved."

Sistine stared at him hard.

And Rob opened his mouth and let the word fall

out. "*Keys,*" he said. Every secret, magic word he had ever known—*tiger* and *cancer* and *Caroline*—every word in his suitcase seemed to fall right out of him when he stood before Sistine.

"What?" she said.

"Keys," he said again. He cleared his throat. "I got the keys to the cage."

"How?"

"Beauchamp," he told her. "He hired me to feed his tiger. And he gave me the keys."

"All right!" said Sistine. "Now all we have to do is open the locks and let him go."

"No," said Rob.

"Are you crazy?" she asked him.

"It ain't safe. It ain't safe for him. My friend Willie May, she had a bird and let it go, and it just got ate up."

"You're not making sense," she told him. "This is a tiger. A tiger, not a bird. And I don't know who Willie May is, and I don't care. You can't stop me from letting this tiger go. I'll do it without the keys. I'll saw the locks off myself."

"Don't," said Rob.

"Don't," she mocked back. And then she spun around and grabbed hold of the cage and shook it the same way Beauchamp had earlier that day.

"I hate this place," she said. "I can't wait for my dad to come and get me. When he gets here, I'm going to make him come out here and set this tiger free. That's the first thing we'll do." She shook the cage harder. "I'll get you out of here," she said to the pacing tiger. "I promise." She rattled the cage as if she were the one who was locked up. The tiger paced back and forth without stopping.

"Don't," said Rob.

But she didn't stop. She shook the cage and beat her head against the chainlink, and then he heard her gasp. He was afraid that maybe she was choking. He went and stood next to her. And he saw that she was crying. *Crying.* Sistine.

He stood beside her, terrified and amazed. When his mother was alive — when he still cried about things — she had been the one who comforted him. She would cup her hand around the back of his neck and say to him, "You go on and cry. I got you. I got good hold of you."

Before Rob could think whether it was right or whether it was wrong, he reached out and put his palm on Sistine's neck. He could feel her pulse, beating in time with the tiger's pacing. He whispered to her the same words his mother had whispered to him. "I got you," he told her. "I got good hold of you."

Sistine cried and cried. She cried as if she would never stop. And she did not tell him to take his hand away.

21

By the time they started walking back to the Kentucky Star, it was dusk. Sistine was not crying, but she wasn't talking, either, not even about letting the tiger go.

"I have to call my mother," she said to him in a tired voice when they got to the motel.

"I'll go with you," said Rob.

She didn't tell him not to, so he walked with her across the parking lot. They were almost to the laundry room when Willie May materialized out of the purple darkness. She was leaning up against her car, smoking a cigarette.

"Boo," she said to Rob.

"Hey," he told her back.

"Somebody following you," she said, jerking her head at Sistine.

"This is Sistine," Rob told her. And then he

turned to Sistine and said, "This is Willie May, the one I was telling you about, the one who had the bird and let it go."

"So what?" said Sistine.

"So nothing," said Willie May. Her glasses winked in the light from the falling Kentucky Star. "So I had me a bird."

"Why are you hanging around in the parking lot trying to scare people?" Sistine asked, her voice hard and mean.

"I ain't trying to scare people," said Willie May.

"Willie May works here," said Rob.

"That's right," said Willie May. She reached into the front pocket of her dress and pulled out a package of Eight Ball gum. "You know what?" she said to Sistine. "I know you. You ain't got to introduce yourself to me. You angry. You got all the anger in the world inside you. I know angry when I meet it. Been angry most of my life."

"I'm not angry," Sistine snapped.

"All right," said Willie May. She opened the package of Eight Ball. "You an angry liar, then. Here you go." She held out a stick of gum to Sistine.

Sistine stared for a long minute at Willie May, and Willie May stared back. The last light of dusk disappeared, and the darkness moved in. Rob held his breath. He wanted desperately for the two of them to like each other. When Sistine finally reached out and took the gum from Willie May, he let his breath go in a quiet *whooosh*.

Willie May nodded at Sistine, and then she extended the pack to Rob. He took a piece and put it in his pocket for later.

Willie May lit another cigarette and laughed. "Ain't that just like God," she said, "throwing the two of you together?" She shook her head. "This boy full of sorrow, keeping it down low in his legs. And you,"—she pointed her cigarette at Sistine—"you all full of anger, got it snapping out of you like lightning. You some pair, that's the truth." She put her arms over her head and stretched and then straightened up and stepped away from the car.

Sistine stared at Willie May, with her mouth open. "How tall are you?" she asked.

"Six feet two," said Willie May. "And I got to get on home. But first, I got some advice for you. I already gave this boy some advice. You ready for yours?"

Sistine nodded, her mouth still open.

"This is it: Ain't nobody going to come and

rescue you," said Willie May. She opened the car door and sat down behind the wheel. "You got to rescue yourself. You understand what I mean?"

Sistine stared at Willie May. She said nothing.

Willie May cranked the engine. Rob and Sistine watched her drive away.

"I think she's a prophetess," said Sistine.

"A what?" Rob said.

"A prophetess," said Sistine. "They're painted all over the Sistine ceiling. They're women who God speaks through."

"Oh," said Rob, "a prophetess." He turned the word over in his mouth. "Prophetess," he said again. He nodded. That sounded right. If God was going to talk through somebody, it made sense to Rob that he would pick Willie May.

22

"You out in the woods with that girl again?" his father asked as soon as Rob stepped into the room.

"Yes, sir," said Rob.

"Look over here, son." His father was standing by Rob's bed.

"Sir?" said Rob. His heart sank. He knew what his father had found: the meat. He had hidden it under his bed until it was time to go and feed the tiger again.

"Where'd this meat come from?" his father asked, pointing at the bloody brown bag.

Without thinking, Rob said, "Beauchamp."

"Beauchamp," his father repeated, low and dark. "Beauchamp. He don't hardly pay me enough to get by, and now he's giving us his rotten meat. He thinks I ain't man enough to put meat on my own table."

Rob wanted to say something, but then he thought of Beauchamp and held his tongue.

"I ought to teach him a lesson," his father said. The cords in his neck stood out like twigs. He kicked the bag of meat. "I ought to," he said. "Making me work for less than nothing, giving us rotten meat."

He went and stood in front of the gun case. He didn't unlock it. He just stood and stared and cracked his knuckles.

"Daddy," said Rob. But he couldn't think of anything to say after that. His mother had known how to calm his father. She would put her hand on his arm or say his name in a soft and reproachful voice, and that would be enough. But Rob didn't know how to do those things. He stood for a minute more, and then he walked over to his bed and grabbed a piece of wood and his knife. As he left the room, his father was still standing at the locked gun case, staring through the glass at the deer-hunting rifle, as if he was trying to will the gun into his hands.

Rob walked to the Kentucky Star sign. He sat down underneath it and leaned up against one of the cold, damp poles and started to work on the wood.

But his head was too full of his father's anger and

Sistine's tears. He couldn't concentrate. He looked up at the dark underside of the sign and recalled lying on a blanket, staring up at a big oak tree. His mother had been on one side of him, and his father, asleep and snoring, had been on the other. He remembered that his mother had taken hold of his hand and pointed up at the sun shining through the leaves of the tree and said, "Look, Rob, I have never in my life seen a prettier color of green. Ain't it perfect?"

"Yes, ma'am," he said, staring at the leaves. "It looks like the original green. The first one God ever thought up."

His mother squeezed his hand hard. "That's right," she said. "The first one God ever thought up. The first-ever green. You and me, we see the world the same."

He concentrated on that green. He let it seep through a crack in his suitcase of not-thoughts and fill up his head with color. He wondered if Willie May's Cricket had been the same bright and original green. That's what he thought about as he carved. And so he wasn't surprised, when he stopped and held the wood away from himself, to see a wing and a beak and a tiny eye. It was Cricket, Willie May's Cricket, coming to life under his knife.

He worked on the bird for a long time, until it looked so real that he half expected it to break into song. When he finally went back to the room, he found his father asleep in the recliner. The gun case was still locked, and the bag of meat was gone. He wouldn't be able to feed the tiger in the morning. He would have to wait until Beauchamp brought him another package.

Rob went and stood over his father and stared down at him. He looked at his heavy hands and the bald spot on his nodding head. He was memorizing him and trying, at the same time, to understand him, to make some sense out of him, out of his anger and his quiet, comparing it to the way he used to sing and smile, when his father jerked awake.

"Hey," he said.

"Hey," Rob said back.

"What time is it?"

"I ain't sure," said Rob. "Late, I guess."

His father sighed. "Go on and get me that leg medicine."

Rob brought him the tube of medicine.

Outside the motel room, the world creaked and sighed. The rain started in again, and his father's hands were gentle as he applied the ointment to Rob's legs.

23

The next morning, Rob put the keys to the tiger cage in one pocket and the wooden bird in the other, and set out looking for Willie May.

He found her in the laundry room, sitting on one of the foldup chairs, smoking a cigarette, and staring into space.

"Hey there," she said to him. "Where's your lady friend at?"

"School," said Rob. "But today's only a half day." He kept his hands in his pockets. Now that he stood before Willie May, he was afraid to give her the bird. What if it was wrong? What if he had carved it wrong and it didn't look anything like the real Cricket?

"What you giving me them shifty-eyed looks for?" Willie May asked.

"I made you something," said Rob quickly, before he lost his nerve.

"Made me something?" said Willie May. "For real?"

"Uh-huh. Close your eyes and hold out your hand."

"I ain't," said Willie May. But she smiled and closed her eyes and put out her enormous hand, palm up. Rob carefully placed the bird in it.

"You can look now," he told her.

She closed her fingers around the little piece of wood, but she didn't open her eyes. She puffed on her cigarette; the long gray ash on the end of it trembled.

"Don't need to look," she finally said. The cigarette ash dropped to the floor. "I know what I got in my hand. It's Cricket."

"But you got to look at it and tell me did I do it right," said Rob.

"I ain't got to do nothing," said Willie May, "except stay black and die." She opened her eyes slowly, as if she was afraid she might frighten the bird into flying away. "This the right bird," she said, nodding her head, "this the one."

"Now you don't got to dream about him no more," said Rob.

"That's right," said Willie May. "Where'd you learn to work a piece of wood like this?"

"My mama," said Rob.

Willie May nodded. "She taught you good."

"Yes, ma'am," said Rob. He stared down at his legs. "I know a wooden bird ain't the same as having a real one."

"It ain't," agreed Willie May. "But it soothes my heart just the same."

"My dad said he ain't got no jobs for me until this afternoon. He said I could help you out this morning."

"Well," said Willie May. She dropped the bird into the front pocket of her dress. "I might could find some way for you to help me."

So Rob spent his morning following Willie May from room to room, stripping the dirty sheets from the beds. And while he worked, the keys jingled in his pocket, and he knew that soon Sistine would be out of school and that she would demand again that he unlock the cage and let the tiger go.

"Where's the prophetess?" Sistine asked him as soon as she stepped off the bus. She was wearing a bright orange dress with pink circles all over it. Her left knee was skinned and bleeding, and her right eye was swollen.

"Huh?" said Rob. He stood and stared at her and wondered how she could get into so many fights in only half a day of school.

"Willie May," said Sistine. "Where is she?"

"She's vacuuming," said Rob.

Sistine started walking purposefully toward the Kentucky Star. She talked to Rob without looking back. "My mother found out that I was wearing your clothes to school," she said. "She took them away from me. I'm in trouble. I'm not supposed to come out here anymore."

"You know," said Rob, "you don't always got to

get in fights. Sometimes, if you don't hit them back, they leave you alone."

She whirled around and faced him. "I want to get in fights," she said fiercely. "I want to hit them back. Sometimes, I hit them first."

"Oh," said Rob.

Sistine turned back around. "I'm going to find the prophetess," she said loudly. "I'm going to ask her what we should do about the tiger."

"You can't ask her about the tiger," said Rob. "Beauchamp said I ain't supposed to tell nobody, especially not Willie May."

Sistine didn't answer him; she started to run. And Rob, to keep up with her, ran too.

They found Willie May vacuuming the shag carpet in room 203. Sistine went up behind her and tapped her on the back. Willie May whirled around with her fist clenched, like a boxer.

"We need some answers," Sistine shouted over the roar of the vacuum cleaner.

Willie May bent down and turned the vacuum cleaner off.

"Well," she said, "look who's here." She kept her hand balled up, as if she was still searching for something to hit.

"What's in your hand?" Sistine asked.

Willie May uncurled her fist and showed Sistine the bird.

"Oh," said Sistine. And Rob realized then why he liked Sistine so much. He liked her because when she saw something beautiful, the sound of her voice changed. All the words she uttered had an *oof* sound to them, as if she was getting punched in the stomach. The sound was in her voice when she talked about the Sistine Chapel and when she looked at the things he carved in wood. It was there when she said the poem about the tiger burning bright, and it was there when she talked about Willie May being a prophetess. Her words sounded the way all those things made him feel, as if the world, the real world, had been punched through, so that he could see something wonderful and dazzling on the other side of it.

"Did Rob make it?" Sistine asked Willie May.

"He did," said Willie May.

"It looks alive. Is it like your bird that you let go?"

"Just about exactly," said Willie May.

"I . . . ," said Sistine. She looked at Willie May. Then she turned and looked at Rob. "We," she said. "We need to ask you something."

"Ask on," said Willie May.

"If you knew about something that was locked up in a cage, something big and beautiful that was locked away unfairly, for no good reason, and you had the keys to the cage, would you let it go?"

Willie May sat down on the bed. A cloud of dust rose up around her. "Lord God," she said. "What you two children got in a cage?"

"It's a tiger," Rob said. He felt like he had to be the one who said it. He was the one who found the tiger. He was the one who had the keys to the cage.

"A what?" said Willie May.

"A tiger," said Sistine.

"Do Jesus!" exclaimed Willie May.

"It's true," said Sistine.

Willie May shook her head. She looked up at the ceiling. She let out her breath in a loud slow hiss of disapproval. "All right," she said. "Why don't you all show me where you got this tiger locked up in a cage?"

25

The three of them walked through the woods in silence. Sistine and Rob chewed Eight Ball gum, and Willie May smoked a cigarette, and nobody said a word.

"Lord God," said Willie May when they came up to the cage. She stared at the pacing animal. "Ain't no reason to doubt the fierceness of God when He make something like that," she said. "Who was the fool that caged this tiger up?"

"He belongs to Beauchamp," Rob told her.

"Beauchamp," said Willie May with disgust. She shook her head. "One person in the world that don't need to be owning no tiger, and that's Beauchamp."

"See?" said Sistine. "It's not right, is it? Just like you told Rob about your bird and how you had to let it go."

"A bird," said Willie May, "that's one thing.

Tiger belonging to Beauchamp is another."

"Tell Rob that he should unlock the cage and let him go," Sistine demanded.

"I ain't," said Willie May. "You got to ask yourself what's going to happen to this tiger after you let him go. How's he going to live?"

Rob was flooded with sad relief. Willie May wasn't going to make him do it. He wasn't going to lose the tiger.

"Panthers live in these woods," argued Sistine. "They survive."

"Used to," said Willie May. "Don't no more."

Sistine put her hands on her hips. "You're not saying what you believe," she accused. "You're not talking like a prophetess."

"That's 'cause I ain't no prophetess," said Willie May. "All I am is somebody speaking the truth. And the truth is: there ain't nothing you can do for this tiger except to let it be."

"It's not right," said Sistine.

"Right ain't got nothing to do with it," muttered Willie May. "Sometimes right don't count."

"I can't wait until my father comes to get me," said Sistine. "He knows what's right. He'll set this tiger free."

Rob looked at Sistine. "Your daddy ain't coming

for you," he said softly, shaking his head, amazed at what he suddenly knew to be the truth.

"My father is coming to get me," Sistine said through tight lips.

"Naw," said Rob sadly. "He ain't. He's a liar. Like your mama said."

"You're the liar," said Sistine in a dark cold voice. Her face was so white that it seemed to glow before him. "And I hate you," she said to him. "Everybody at school hates you, too. Even the teachers. You are a sissy. I hope I never ever see you again."

She turned and walked away, and Rob stood and considered her words. He felt them on his skin like shards of broken glass. He was afraid to move. He was afraid of how deep they might go inside him.

"She don't mean it," said Willie May. "She don't mean none of what she say right now."

Rob shrugged. He bent and scratched his legs as hard as he could. He scratched and scratched, digging his nails in deep, trying to get to the bottom of the itch that was always there.

"Stop it," Willie May told him.

Rob looked up at her.

"Let me tell you something," she said. "I would love to see this tiger rise on up out of this cage.

Yes, uh-huh. I would like to see him rise on up and attack Beauchamp; serve him right for keeping a wild animal locked up, putting you in the middle of this, giving you the keys to this cage. Come on." She grabbed hold of Rob's hand. "Let's get on up out of here."

As they walked back to the Kentucky Star, Rob thought about what Willie May had said about the tiger rising on up. It reminded him of what she had said about his sadness needing to rise up. And when he thought about the two things together, the tiger and his sadness, the truth circled over and above him and then came and landed lightly on his shoulder. He knew what he had to do.

He left Willie May at the motel and went down the
highway.

"Sistine!" he shouted as he ran. "Sistine!" he
screamed.

And miraculously, he saw her—her orange dress
with the pink polka dots—glowing on the horizon.
Sistine Bailey.

"Hey," he shouted. "Sistine. I got something to
tell you."

"I'm not talking to you," she shouted back. But
she stopped. She turned around. She put her hands
on her hips.

He ran faster.

"I come to tell you about the tiger," he said when
he caught up with her.

"What about him?"

"I'm fixing to let him go," said Rob.

Sistine squinted her eyes at him. "You won't do it," she said.

"Yes, I will," he told her. He reached into his pocket and pulled out the keys and held them in front of her, proudly, as if he had just conjured them out of thin air, as if they had never existed before. "I'm going to do it," he said. "I'm going to do it for you."

"Whoooooeeee!!!!!" somebody screamed, and Rob turned and saw Beauchamp come speeding right toward them in his red jeep.

"Oh no," whispered Rob.

"Is it him?" Sistine whispered.

Rob nodded.

Beauchamp pulled over to the side of the road, spraying mud and water everywhere.

"You out getting your exercise?" he hollered.

Rob shrugged.

"Speak up," roared Beauchamp. He got out of the jeep and came toward them. Rob quickly pocketed the keys. His heart thumped once, loudly, as if it was cautioning him to keep quiet, and then it went back to beating normally.

"Well, looky here," said Beauchamp when he saw

Sistine. "You out chasing girls. Is that it? Man after my own heart. This your girlfriend?" Beauchamp pounded Rob on the back.

"No, sir," said Rob. He looked at Sistine. She was staring so hard at Beauchamp that Rob was afraid the man might burst into flames.

"I got more goods for you," Beauchamp said. "I left 'em back at the motel with Ida Belle."

"Yes, sir," said Rob.

"What's your name, little thing?" Beauchamp said, turning to Sistine.

Rob's heart gave another warning thump. Lord only knew what Sistine would say to Beauchamp.

But Sistine, as always, surprised him. She smiled sweetly at Beauchamp. "Sissy," she said.

"Well, that's pretty," said Beauchamp. "That's the kind of name worth running down the road after." He leaned over to Rob. "Remember what we got going. You're keeping your manly secrets, ain't you?"

"Yes, sir," said Rob.

Beauchamp winked. His toothpick wiggled.

"I got me some business in town," he said. He squeezed Rob's shoulder hard and then took his hand away. "You and your girlfriend stay out of trouble, now, you hear?"

"Yes, sir," said Rob.

Beauchamp swaggered back to the jeep, and Rob and Sistine stood together and watched him get in it and roar down the highway.

"He's afraid," said Sistine. "He's afraid of the tiger. That's why he's making you feed him."

Rob nodded. That was another truth he had known without knowing it, the same as he had known that Sistine's father was not coming back. He must, he realized, know somewhere, deep inside him, more things than he had ever dreamed of.

"I'm sorry," he said. "What I said about your daddy, I'm sorry."

"I don't want to talk about my father," said Sistine.

"Maybe he *is* coming to get you."

"He's not coming to get me." Sistine tossed her head. "And I don't care. It doesn't matter. What matters is the tiger. Let's go. Let's go set him free."

27

The first key slid into the first lock so smoothly that it made Rob dizzy with amazement. It was going to be so easy to let the tiger go.

"Hurry," Sistine said to him. "Hurry up. Get the other locks."

He opened the second lock and the third. And then he took them off one by one and handed them to Sistine, who laid them on the ground.

"Now open the door," she said.

Rob's heart pounded and fluttered in his chest. "What if he eats us?" he asked.

"He won't," said Sistine. "He'll leave us alone out of gratitude. We're his emancipators."

Rob flung the door wide.

"Get out of the way," he shouted, and they both jumped back from the door and waited. But the tiger ignored them. He continued to pace back and forth in the cage, oblivious to the open door.

"Go on," Rob said to him.

"You're free," Sistine whispered.

But the tiger did not even look in the direction of the door.

Sistine crept forward and grabbed hold of the cage. She shook it.

"Get out!" she screamed. "Come on," she said, turning to Rob, "help me. Help me get him out."

Rob grabbed hold of the fence and shook it. "Get," he said.

The tiger stopped pacing and turned to stare at them both clinging like monkeys to the cage.

"Go on!" Rob shouted, suddenly furious. He shook the cage harder. He yelled. He put his head back and howled, and he saw that the sky above them was thick with clouds, and that made him even angrier. He yelled louder; he shouted at the dark sky. He shook the cage as hard as he could.

Sistine put a hand on his arm. "Shhh," she said. "He's leaving. Watch."

As they stared, the tiger stepped with grace and delicacy out of the cage. He put his nose up and sniffed. He took one tiny step and then another.

Then he stopped and stood still. Sistine clapped her hands, and the tiger turned and looked back at them both, his eyes blazing And then he started to run.

He ran so fast, it looked to Rob like he was flying. His muscles moved like a river; it was hard to believe that a cage had ever contained him. It didn't seem possible.

The tiger went leaping through the grass, moving farther and farther away from Rob and Sistine. He looked like the sun, rising and setting again and again. And watching him go, Rob felt his own heart rising and falling, beating in time.

28

"Oh," said Sistine, in that voice that Rob loved. "See," she said, "that was the right thing. That was the right thing to do."

Rob nodded. But in his mind, he saw a flash of green. He remembered what happened to Cricket.

"What?" said Sistine, turning to him. "What are you thinking about?"

Rob shook his head. "Nothing," he told her.

"*Roberrttt.*" The sound of his name came floating to them from the direction of the motel.

"That's my dad," he said, confused. "That's my dad calling me."

And then they heard Willie May. "Do Jesus!" she screamed, her voice high and wild.

And then there was the crack of a gun.

They both stood still, stunned and silent. And

when Willie May came running out from under the pine trees and saw them, she stopped. "Thank you, Jesus," she said, looking up at the sky. "Two whole children. Thank you. Come here," she said. She opened her arms. "Come to me."

Rob started walking toward her. He wanted to tell her that she was wrong. He wanted to tell her that he did not feel whole. But he did not have the energy or the heart to say anything; all he could manage was putting one foot in front of the other. All he could do was keep walking toward Willie May.

Willie May led them back. And when Rob saw the tiger on the ground and his father standing over it, holding the rifle, he felt something rise up in him, an anger as big and powerful as the tiger. Bigger.

"You killed him," he said to his father.

"I had to," his father said.

"That was my tiger!" Rob screamed. "You killed him! You killed my tiger!" He ran at his father and attacked him. He beat him with his fists. He kicked him. But his father stood like a wall. He held the gun up over his head and kept his eyes open and took each hit without blinking.

And Rob saw that hitting wasn't going to be

enough. So he did something he thought he would never do. He opened his suitcase. And the words sprang out of it, coiled and explosive.

"I wish it had been you!" he screamed. "I wish it had been you that died! I hate you! You ain't the one I need. I need her! I need her!"

The world, and everything in it, seemed to stop moving.

He stared at his father.

His father stared at him.

"Say her name!" Rob screamed into the silence. "You say it!"

"Caroline," his father whispered, with the gun still over his head, with his eyes still open.

And with that word, with the small sound of his mother's name, the world lurched back into motion; like an old merry-go-round, it started to spin again. His father put the gun down and pulled Rob to him.

"Caroline," his father whispered. "Caroline, Caroline, Caroline."

Rob buried his face in his father's shirt. It smelled like sweat and turpentine and green leaves. "I need her," Rob said.

"I need her, too," said his father, pulling Rob closer. "But we don't got her. Neither one of us. What we got, all we got, is each other. And we got to learn to make do with that."

"I ain't going to cry," Rob said, shutting his eyes, but the tears leaked out of him, anyway. Then they came in a rush and he couldn't stop. He cried from somewhere deep inside of himself, from the place where his mother had been, the same place that the tiger had been and was gone from now.

Rob looked up and saw his father wiping tears from his own eyes.

"All right," said his father, holding Rob tight. "That's all right," he said. "You're okay."

When Rob finally looked up again, he saw Willie May holding Sistine like she was a baby, rocking her and saying *shhhh.*

Willie May stared back at him. "Don't think you gonna start pounding on me now," she said.

"No, ma'am," said Rob. He wiped the back of his hand across his nose and slid out of his father's arms.

"I went and got your daddy," Willie May told Rob as she swayed back and forth, rocking Sistine. "I figured out what you was gonna do. And there ain't no telling what that tiger would've done once he got out of that cage. I went and got your daddy, so he could save you."

"Yes, ma'am," said Rob.

He went and stood over the open-eyed tiger. The bullet hole in his head was red and small; it didn't look big enough to kill him.

"Go ahead and touch him," said Sistine.

Rob looked up. She was standing beside him. Her dress was twisted and wrinkled. Her eyes were red. Rob stared at her and she nodded. So he knelt and put out a hand and placed it on the tiger's head. He felt the tears rise up in him again.

Sistine crouched down next to him. She put her hand on the tiger, too. "He was so pretty," she said. "He was one of the prettiest things I have ever seen."

Rob nodded.

"We have to have a funeral for him," Sistine said. "He's a fallen warrior. We have to bury him right."

Rob sat down next to the tiger and ran his hand over the rough fur again and again while the tears traveled down his cheeks and dropped onto the ground.

Rob and his father worked with shovels to dig a hole that was deep enough and wide enough and dark enough to hold the tiger. And the whole time, it rained.

"We got to say some words over him," said Willie May when the hole was done and the tiger was in it. "Can't cover up nothing without saying some words."

"I'll say the poem," said Sistine. She folded her hands in front of her and looked down at the ground. "'Tiger, tiger, burning bright / in the forests of the night,'" she recited.

Rob closed his eyes.

"'What immortal hand or eye / Could frame thy fearful symmetry?'" Sistine continued. "'In what distant deeps or skies / Burnt the fire of thine eyes? / On what wings dare he aspire?'"

To Rob, the words sounded like music, but better. His eyes filled up with tears again. He worried that now that he had started crying, he might never stop.

"That's all I remember," Sistine said after a minute. "There's more to it, but I can't remember it all. You say something now, Rob," she said.

"I don't got nothing to say," said Rob, "except for, I loved him."

"Well," said Willie May. "What I got to say is I ain't had good experiences with animals in cages." She reached into her dress pocket and took out the wooden bird and bent down and laid it on top of the tiger. "That ain't nothing," she said to the tiger, "just a little bird to keep you company." She stepped back, away from the grave.

Rob's father cleared his throat. He hummed softly, and Rob thought he was going to sing, but instead, he shook his head and said, "I had to shoot him. I'm sorry, but I had to shoot him. For Rob."

Rob leaned into his father, and it felt, for a minute, like his father leaned back. Then Rob picked up his shovel and started covering the tiger with dirt. As he filled the grave, something danced and flickered on his arm. Rob stared at it, wondering what it was. And then he recognized it. It was the sun. Showing up in time for another funeral.

"I'm sorry I made you do it," Sistine said to Rob when he was done. "He wouldn't be dead if I hadn't made you do it."

"It's all right," Rob said. "I ain't sorry about what I did."

"We can make a headstone for him," said Sistine. "And we can bring flowers and put them on his grave—fresh ones, every day." She slipped her hand into his. "I didn't mean what I said before, about you being a sissy. And I don't hate you. You're my best friend."

The whole way back to the Kentucky Star, Rob held on to Sistine's hand. He marveled at what a small hand it was and how much comfort there was in holding on to it.

And he marveled, too, at how different he felt inside, how much lighter, as if he had set something heavy down and walked away from it, without bothering to look back.

30

That night, his father sang to Rob as he put the medicine on his legs. He sang the song about mining for gold, the one that he used to sing with Rob's mother. When he was done with the medicine and the song, he cleared his throat and said, "Caroline loved that song."

"Me too," Rob told him. "I like it too."

His father stood up. "You're going to have to tell Beauchamp that you was the one that let that tiger go."

"Yes, sir," said Rob.

"I'll tell him I was the one who shot him, but you got to admit to letting him go."

"Yes, sir," said Rob again.

"I might could lose my job over it," his father said.

"I know it," Rob told him. But he wasn't afraid. He thought about Beauchamp's shaking hands.

Beauchamp was the coward. He knew that now. "I thought I would tell him I could work for him to pay for what I done."

"You can offer him up some reasonable kind of solution," said his father, "but it don't mean he'll go for it. There ain't no predicting Beauchamp. Other than to say he's going to be mad."

Rob nodded.

"And on Monday," his father continued, "I aim to call that principal and tell him you're going back to school. I ain't messing around with taking you to more doctors. You're going back and that's that."

"Yes, sir," said Rob. He didn't mind the thought of going back to school. School was where Sistine would be.

His father cleared his throat. "It's hard for me to talk about your mama. I wouldn't never have believed that I could miss somebody the way I miss her. Saying her name pains me." He bent his head and concentrated on putting the cap on the tube of medicine. "But I'll say it for you," he said. "I'll try on account of you."

Rob looked at his father's hands. They were the hands that had held the gun that shot the tiger. They were the hands that put the medicine on his legs. They were the hands that had held him when he cried. They were complicated hands, Rob thought.

"You want some macaroni and cheese for dinner?" his father asked, looking back up at Rob.

"That sounds all right," said Rob. "Macaroni and cheese sounds real good."

That night, Rob dreamed he and Sistine were standing at the grave of the tiger. They were watching and waiting. He didn't know for what. But then he saw a flutter of green wings and he understood. It was the wooden bird, only he wasn't made of wood, he was real. And he flew up out of the tiger's grave, and they chased him, laughing and bumping into each other. They tried to catch him. But they couldn't. The bird flew higher and higher until he disappeared into a sky that looked just like the Sistine ceiling. In his dream, Rob stood and stared up at the sky, admiring all the figures and the colors, watching as the bird disappeared into them.

"See?" said Sistine in his dream. "I told you it was like fireworks."

He woke up smiling, staring at the ceiling of the motel room.

"Guess what?" his father called to him from outside.

"What?" said Rob back.

"There ain't a cloud in the sky," said his father, "that's what."

Rob nodded. He lay in bed and watched the sun poke its way through his curtain. He thought about Sistine and the tiger he wanted to make for her. He thought about what kind of wood he would use and how big he would make the tiger. He thought about how happy Sistine would be when she saw it.

He lay in bed and considered the future, and outside his window, the tiny neon Kentucky Star rose and fell and rose and fell, competing bravely with the light of the morning sun.